Yahloni and the Matanah
Written by Ameerah Bat Yah
Illustrated by Tajha Alston

I AM Media Books

Children's Books Imprint

ISBN: 978-1-951667-02-3

Published by I AM Media Books, Michigan, USA

Media to Awaken the World!

www.iammediabooks.com

One day Yahloni came to her mom with these words, "Mom, I have no talents." Puzzled her mom asked, "What do you mean?"

"Well, do you know Yahsai from Shabbat class? She can draw very well and she makes beautiful drawings to Yah. I can't even draw stick figures."

"Ok," said Yahloni's mom.

Yahloni continued: "Have you heard Laileeyah blow the shofar at all the feast?"

"Yael reads from Torah as if she's face to face with Yah. Yaakov writes wonderful stories and recites poetry as if he's Melek Dawid."

Yahloni's mom listened intently as Yahloni carried on about the talented people she knew. Yahloni groaned and moaned about how talented she was not and how much more talent her friends and family had.

"All I can do is whistle." Yahloni plopped down on the couch near her mom and let out a gigantic sigh. She poked out her lips and grunted, "What good is whistling? That's no talent at all . I will never whistle again!"

"Are you done my Yaphah Baht Yah?" asked her mother.

"I guess. I just don't get why Yah, who is fair and just, would give my friends such beautiful talents. Some of them have three or four, or even endless talents. Yah gave me nothing but a whistle!" complained Yahloni.

"So,what are you going to do with it?" asked her mom.

"With what?" retorted Yahloni.

"Your talent," said her mom excitedly.

Yahloni looked at her mom in disbelief, with her mouth gaped open. "Mom, weren't you listening to anything I just said?" Yahloni flustered.

"Yes, of course I was my Yaphah Baht Yah. And again I ask, what are you going to do with the talent of whistling Yah blessed you with?"

"Mom, whistling is not a talent!" cried Yahloni.

"Wait are you trying to tell me whistling is a blessing from Almighty Yah? That's silly mom! " Yahloni laughed. "What can I do with whistling?" she continued to complain.

"Sit up. Let me tell you a story. It's called the Matanah."

"Oh mom, you just made that up," scoffed Yahloni.

"Hush up and listen child."

"There was a man going on a trip to a far away place. He planned to be away for a while. Before he left, he needed to make sure his posessions would be taken care of. So, he called three of his servants. He gave the first servant five tunics, the second two sheep and the last a single seed.

'Maccabeus!' the master called to the first servant.

'Yes Master?' answered Maccabeus.

'I am going on a trip, I do not know when I will return. I leave in your care my five tunics. Tend to them for me while I am away.'

'Yonas!'the master bellowed. 'I leave you with my two sheep. Care for them while I am gone.'
'Yes Master.' Yonas said with joy.

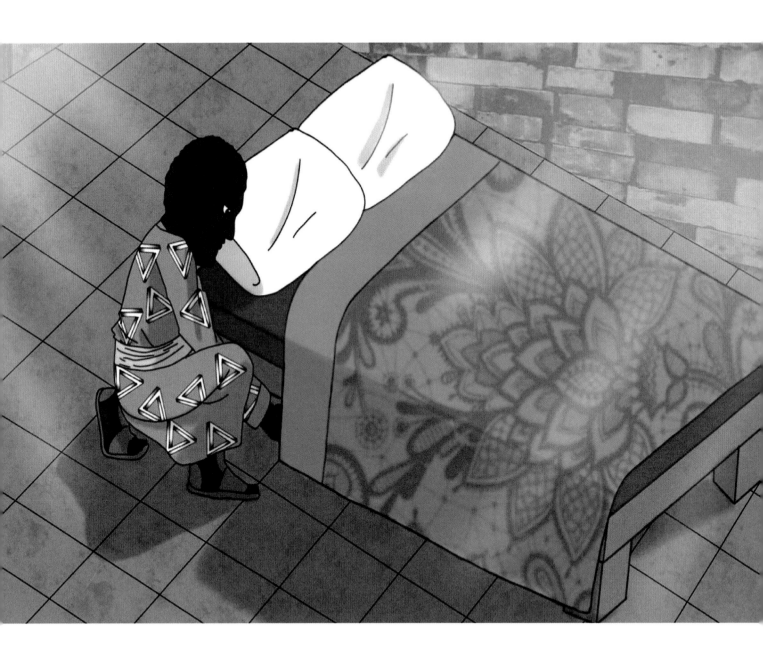

"Come Yochanan!" the master bellowed as he placed a single seed in his hand. Yochanan took the seed and walked away.

'One little seed?' He muttered to himself. 'What am I supposed to do with one little seed? Why didn't my master give me something useful? Like garments! Look at all those beautiful garments he entrusted to Maccabeus. I see those two healthy sheep the master gave to Yonas. But to me he gives ahat tsair zera, one insignificant seed,' Yochanan scoffed. What type of matanah is this?'

Yochanan looked at the seed once more and threw it on the floor in his bedroom. The seed rolled under his bed where it stayed. The days turned into months, then years. In all the time that passed, Yochanan never touched the seed. He grew bitter as he watched the two other servants prosper with their gifts."

"Maccabeus took the five garments his master left him and sold them. With the money he purchased a sewing machine, some fabric and other sewing equipment to expand his business. When the master came back, he returned the five garments he was given and gave him five extra. "The master saw Maccebus was not only faithful but also good for Yithron."

"With the two sheep the master gave Yonas he made coats with the wool. He sold the coats and bought two more sheep. Each set of sheep bore a lamb. The few sheep multiplied in Yonas' care. Before you could say 'Baaaaaaaaa' Yonas had a whole herd of sheep. Upon his master's return, Yonas gave back four sheep to his master as a way of saying todah for the matanah.
'Yahuah baruhk you Yonas, here are two more sheep for your faithfulness,' expressed the master."

"When Yochanan heard of his master's return, he quickly ran to retrieve the seed his master gave him. As he walked to his room he murmured, 'I know Yonas and Maccabeus multiplied what the master gave them, but I was only given one seed. I'm sure the master didn't expect me to do anything with that. He should be happy I stil have it.' When the master returned, he was greeted with the one little seed he left in Yochanan's care. The master took the seed and walked away."

"Yochanan called to the master" Bevakasha adon, excuse me master! That's it? Not even a todah? Nothing? You gave unto the others plenty and upon your return you gave them even more. Yet me you have given very little, and even still you come to take that very thing away. Okay Master, what gives? Why do you hate me so? I have kept the seed safe all these many years. Thinking maybe my master would be proud, considering he gave me nothing to work with. 'AHAT TSAIR ZERA, ONE INSIGNIFICANT SEED!' Yochanan hysterically shouted at his master as he pumped his fist and stamped his feet. 'I just dont understand why you gave everyone else such beautiful gifts, but only gave me one measly seed,' he continued to shout."

"The master turned around and said in a calm but assertive voice. 'Yochanan I do not hate you, I love you exceedingly, but you have missed the lesson in all this my son. Because you coveted your brother's gifts and despised your very own, you missed out on your own blessing. You failed to realize I gave you the greatest matanah of all.'

'You should have taken the energy you used trying to figure out why I gave the others what I did not give you and planted the seed in the ground. You could have watered the seed and watched it grow into a plant which bears a fruit called tomatoes. Then you would harvested not one tomato, but many tomatoes and many more seeds! Had you been faithful and thankful, you could have harvested those tomatoes, extracted the seeds and eventually had a whole crop of seeds, maybe even your own tomato farm.'

"But you were so busy looking at others' gifts and despising your own, you couldn't make use of your own beautiful matanah. Had you been faithful over the little, you would have been blessed with more. Since you weren't even grateful for what you had, it will be taken away.' When the master was done speaking he turned and walked away. The perplexed servant stood there with his mouth gaped open in astonishment. For the first time in his life he could see clearly Yochanan made up his mind he would never again despise anything given to him."

"From that day forward the murmuring servant worked diligently with his hands as a tomato farmer. Yochanan brought forth a plentious harvest in due season with joy, And guess what? Once he learned how to use his gift, he was a natural."

"Wow mom, I completely understand. Instead of looking at other people's gifts and complaining about what I can't do, I should focus on what I can do because I never know what may come of it. Thanks, that was a great story!" exclaimed Yahloni.

Yahloni got up and walked off whistling a happy melody. She turned back to her mom and said "I may have a talent after all."

Glossary

Matanah	Gift
Melek	King
Yaphah	Beautiful
Baht	Daughter
Yah	Yahuah
Ahat	One

Tsair	Insignificant
Zera	Seed
Yithron	Profit
Todah	Thank You
Baruhk	Bless
Bevakasha	Excuse Me
Adon	Master

Covet: To desire wrongfully, inordinately, or without due regard for the rights of others: to covet another's property. To wish for, especially eagerly.
https://www.dictionary.com/browse/covet

About the Author

Ameerah Bat Yah is a mother of 7; doula, artist, songwriter and Author-preneur. She is a stay at home mom who homeschools. She enjoys teaching and encouraging others to live according to Yahuah's word.

Ameerah Bat Yah

Made in the USA
Middletown, DE
06 June 2020